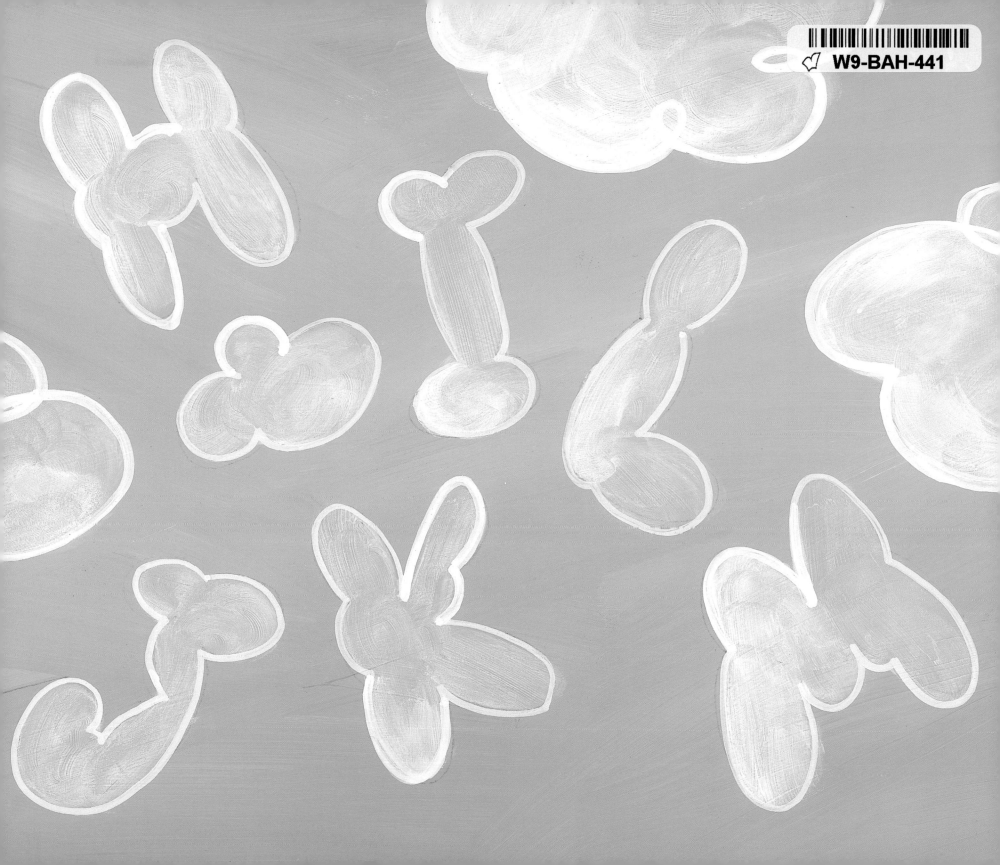

F is for Fireflies

God's Summertime Alphabet

By Kathy-jo Wargin

Illustrated by Linda Bronson

ZONDERkidz

ZONDERVAN.com/
AUTHORTRACKER
follow your favorite authors

ZONDERKIDZ

F Is for Fireflies
Copyright © 2011 by Kathy-jo Wargin
Illustrations copyright © 2011 by Linda Bronson

Requests for information should be addressed to:
Zonderkidz, Grand Rapids, Michigan 49530

Library of Congress Cataloging-in-Publication Data

Wargin, Kathy-jo.
    F is for fireflies / by Kathy-jo Wargin ; illustrated by Linda Bronson.
        p. cm.
    Summary: Presents rhyming sentences for each letter of the alphabet that remind the reader of
God's blessings in summer.
    ISBN 978-0-310-71663-1 (hardcover)
    [1. Stories in rhyme. 2. Summer—Fiction. 3. God—Fiction. 4. Alphabet.] I. Bronson, Linda, ill. II. Title.
PZ8.3.W2172Fai 2011
[E]—dc22   2008044102

Editor: Barbara Herndon
Art direction: Jody Langley

Printed in China
11 12 13 14 15 /LPC/ 10 9 8 7 6 5 4 3 2 1

To the spirit of summer and all the beauty it brings.

—K.W.

For Charlie and Frannie.

—L.B.

A is for Anchor

Lift up your **A**nchor; the sunshine is here.
It's time for the blessings of God's summer cheer.

B is for Boat

Summer brings **B**oats
that set sail in the breeze.
The water reminds us
that God calms the seas.

C is for Castle

Let's find a beach
    to build Castles of sand.
God tells us kindness
    means lending a hand.

D is for Daisy

Let's pick some **D**aisies
of yellow and white.
The center reminds us
of God's pure delight!

E is for Everything

For God made the summer—he made Everything!
He made fish swim and whip-poor-wills sing.

F is for Fireflies

God made the **F**ireflies
light up the night,
a flash and a flicker—
his love is so bright!

G is for Garden

God made the **G**ardens,
and we help them grow,
weeding and watering
row after row.

H is for Hat

The sun rises high, and we feel very hot!
It's time for a **H**at and a cool shady spot.

I is for Inchworm

We spy an **I**nchworm,
   a friend to be treasured.
Each step reminds us
   God's love can't be measured.

J is for Jump rope

It's time to Jump rope. Let's be quick on our feet.
We'll try to jump fast without skipping a beat.

K is for Kickball

Or we can play **K**ickball, a fun summer game.
We are all friends, and God knows us by name.

L is for Ladybug

Summer brings **L**adybugs
dressed up in spots.
Sometimes with few,
sometimes with lots!

M is for Meadow

Let's walk through the **M**eadow
and smell the fresh air.
Like wind through the grasses,
God's always there.

N is for Nature

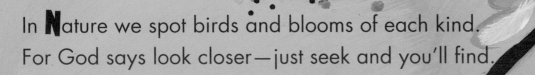

In **N**ature we spot birds and blooms of each kind.
For God says look closer—just seek and you'll find.

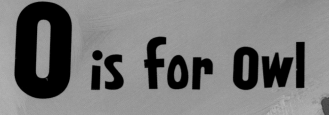# O is for Owl

Owls perch high with their big watching eyes.
Remember that God wants us all to be wise.

P is for Picnic

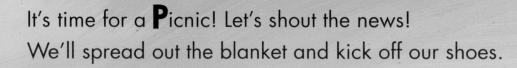

It's time for a **P**icnic! Let's shout the news!
We'll spread out the blanket and kick off our shoes.

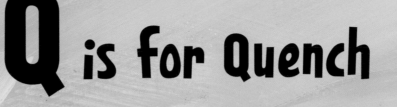 Q is for Quench

Let's **Q**uench our thirst
with fresh lemonade.
It always tastes better
when it is homemade.

10¢

R is for Rainbow

Rainbows in summer are God's way to say
that after the rain comes a brilliant new day.

S is for Swim

Let's go for a **S**wim—the water feels cool
when we jump in a lake or wade in a pool.

T is for Tire

Grandpa's old **T**ire swing
hangs from the tree.
A warm summer breeze
makes it fun to soar free.

U is for Universe

We sleep under stars
while admiring above,
the Universe calling to all,
"God is love."

V is for Vacation

It's time for **V**acation—we've waited all year.
Wherever we travel, we know God is near.

W is for Wave

Let's **W**ave to new friends as we travel along,
and make the time pass with a story or song.

X is for eXploring

We'll go eXploring;
    there's so much to do—
hiking and biking,
    enjoying the view.

Y is for Yellow

The Yellow sun's setting;
the day's nearly done.
It's time to go home,
but we've had so much fun.

Z is for ZZZs

The hammock is waiting below the best trees.
Let's swing in the sunset before we catch **Z**ZZs.

From **A**nchors to **B**eaches
and summery things,
may you find the blessings that
God's summer brings.

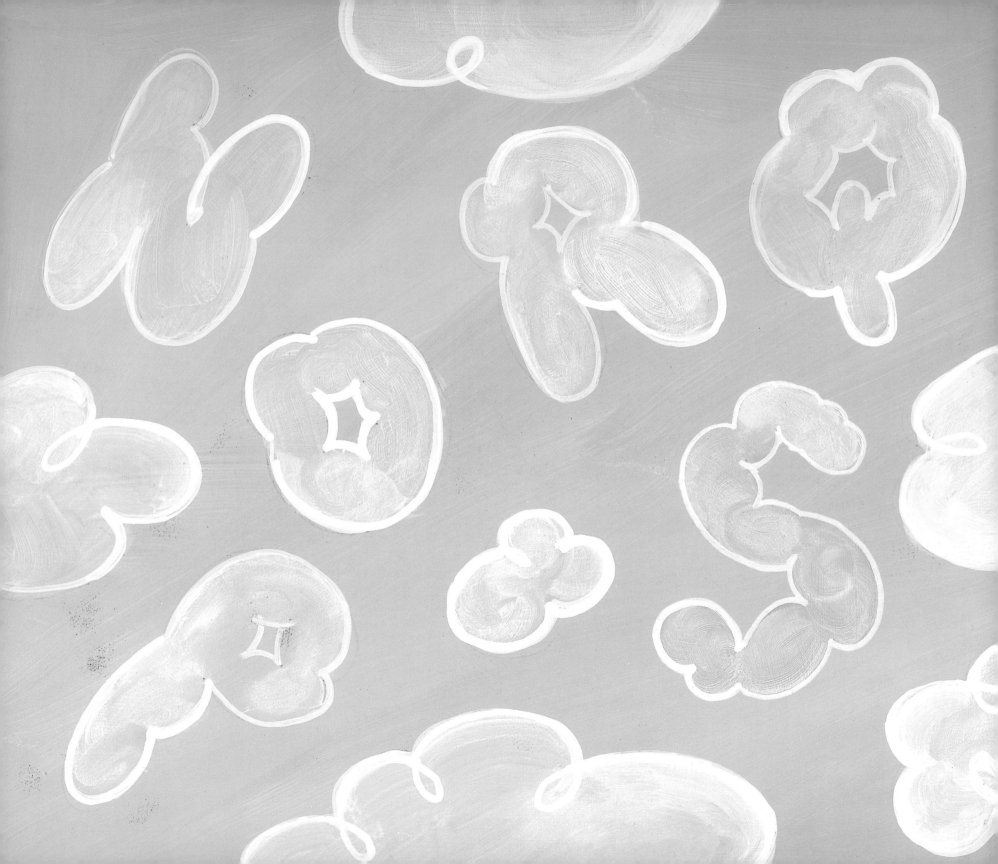